BIG RED

The Father of Santa's Reindeer

Special thanks to

Bob & Diane Hanley, Leah Watson-Thomas

and all who keep the Christmas Spirit year round!

Written by

Danny and Adrian Cennamo

Illustrations by

Brittany Hunter

BIG RED

The Father of Santa's Reindeer

There was a time when we believed in Fairies, Unicorns, Dragons, and Wishes. It was a time when magic was real and things did not have to be proven; we just believed!

During such a time, high in the mountains of northern Europe, in an area of forest outside the village of Reinland lived a herd of deer. These weren't just any deer; they were a special breed of deer. Being larger and stronger than your average deer, they were chosen guardians of the Reinland Forest. On a snowy winter night, a fawn was born exactly at midnight. He wasn't to be just any deer and didn't look exactly like the others. You see, he was born with a bright, shiny red fur coat. Seeing his shiny red fur, his parents decided to call him Big Red.

As a young buck, Big Red showed great strength and agility. His task when he was old enough was to help clear the old forest trees that had died, to make room for the new growth forest. Big Red became a friend to the forest creatures, and they all loved Big Red. He was there for anyone who might have need of help. As the years went on, Big Red grew taller and stronger than all the deer in the Reinland Forest. Being different from other deer, huge and with bright red fur, he felt that there was some reason for this, but didn't know why.

One night he awoke to the sound of a voice telling him, "Big Red, you must follow the bright star in the sky. It will lead you to your destiny."

That morning he told his parents what he had heard and about the new bright star he saw in the sky. Surprised, his parents revealed they had heard the Angel as well. In the evening as the sun went down and the stars began to shine, Big Red said his goodbyes and headed out in the direction of the star. This star was bright, casting a beautiful glow across the land, which made it easy for Big Red to see the path.

Traveling by night and resting by day, Big Red moved down the mountain. On the 7th day at sunrise the clouds parted and the sun cast a beam of light through the clouds. This beam shone upon a perfect fur pine tree, illuminating it. He stopped and stared at this tree. He knew instantly he was supposed to bring it with him. Why he had to do this, he didn't know. Pushing on the trunk of the tree as hard as he could, it started to give way and pull the roots from the ground. He wrapped the roots in a blanket and dipped it in the creek that was along the path. He knew by doing this, he could keep the roots moist and the tree fresh. When he finished, he went to a nearby tree, broke off some large branches and began to eat the bark, leaving a clean smooth branch behind. After eating, Big Red found a place to lie down. He fell into a deep sleep and dreamt.

When he awoke, he remembered a dream he had about following the star. In this dream, he saw a town with many people visiting, but did not know where this town was or why the people were there. After grazing on the grass that had laid under him, thanks to his body heat melting the snow, he hoisted the tree onto his back and set off following the bright star that was just above the horizon. Looking ahead at the path, he could see the valley below, and he knew he was almost at the bottom of the mountain.

As dawn arrived and the sky turned from a dark blue to a beautiful cascade of colors, he knew it was time to stop and rest. He removed the fur pine tree from his back. He was setting it aside when he heard a voice.

"Hello there, Mr. Deer. I must say I have never seen a deer like you before, so big and shinning, so bright red."

Turning his head quickly, he jumped a bit when he saw the young man standing behind him. Big Red spoke.

"You startled me, Sir, and who might you be? Wait! How is it I can understand what it is you are saying?"

The young man answered, "My name is Nicholas, from the village of Reinland. Now, as far as you and me understanding each other, I believe it has to do with the star we seem to both be following. I believe this star is magic, divine even. You see, ever since I heard the Angel telling me to follow this star I have been able to understand all the forest animals. Magic? Destiny? Maybe a miracle, I think. I know this star is divine, and there are great things to come."

Big Red looked at Nicholas and said, "Miracle, huh? What makes you think that?"

"Well…," Nicholas paused, thinking, and then continued, "for example, since I started this journey I can speak with the animals and have been finding these large branches on the path that are in my cart." Nicholas pointed to the branches in the cart and continued, "All of these branches are stripped of bark."

Big Red said, "I don't think that is so amazing. I ate the bark off those branches and left them near the path."

Nicholas looked at Big Red smiled and said, "Yes, I believe they are for me. You see, I carve toys for the children of my village, and to find a piece of wood with the bark off saves me a lot of time. To me, that's amazing!" Nicholas asked, "You know my name, Mr. Deer, so what is yours?"

"Big Red is my name, Sir."

"I should have guessed it by your size and color," he said. "It is wonderful to meet you, Big Red. Since we are traveling on the same quest, we should travel together."

"I would love the company," replied Big Red.

Since it was already dawn, they set up camp, ate and rested so they could be ready for the next part of their journey.

Weeks went by. They traveled by night, always following the star, and slept by day. During that time, Nicholas made his cart larger so the fur tree could be placed on the back of it. He built a bench for himself up front, and made a harness for Big Red so he could pull the cart. As they followed the star, they learned all about each other, their families and friends. Big Red told Nicholas that he was from a special herd of deer that were larger than the regular deer. He explained that his herd were the guardians of the Reinland forest. Nicholas explained to Big Red how much the children of his village loved the toys he made. He told Big Red of his friends and that he had no family yet, but considered all the children of the village his family.

Nicholas asked Big Red, "Do all the deer of your herd have bright red fur?"

"No, I am the only one," Big Red answered.

They traveled through the great nations of Europe, around the Mediterranean Sea, south past the city of Jerusalem and found themselves in a town where hundreds of people gathered to be counted in a census.

The star they had been following was directly overhead, and they knew they had

reached their destination. Yet, they still did not know why they were there.

Knocking on the door of an Inn, which had a large barn next to it, Nicholas asked the

Inn Keeper if he had room.

The Inn Keeper answered, "No, we are all filled up due to the census."

As Nicholas turned away to leave, the Inn Keeper noticed his cart with

carpenter tools and wood in it.

He asked, "Are you a carpenter?"

"I am," Nicholas replied.

The Inn Keeper thought a moment and said, "If you are willing to do repairs to the

barn, you and your deer, if that is what it is, may sleep there."

"Thank you, we will do excellent repairs for you," Nicholas said. Nicholas and

Big Red moved their things into the barn. Big Red took the fur pine tree and placed

it in the corner of the barn. Together, for the next few days they worked hard

repairing the roof, walls and stalls. When they finished Nicholas took the remainder of the wood and made hay troughs for the front of each stall. They put

fresh hay in each and made them ready for the animals. Nicholas realized he made

one too many. Looking at that trough, a manger, he felt it was special and was

made for a reason. He filled it with fresh hay and placed it under the fur pine tree.

Big Red and Nicholas put away their tools, ate and went to sleep. During the night

they were awakened by the sound of people entering the barn. As they looked on

from the corner where they had been sleeping, they saw a man and a woman, who

was expecting a baby, enter the barn.

As the people walked to the other corner near the fur tree, Nicholas

noticed the man helping the lady down onto a bed of hay. She was about to give

birth. As they watched the Child being born, they saw a bright light like the star

they had followed enter through the roof of the barn. An Angel appeared and

spoke. His voice could be heard throughout the world.

"Be not afraid, for behold, I bring you good tidings of great joy, which shall be to all people; for there is born to you this day in the city of David, a Savior, who is Christ the Lord. And this is the sign unto you; you shall find a Babe wrapped in swaddling clothes, and lying in a manger."

Nicholas and Big Red noticed that this special Child was placed in the manger they had built. They knew now He was the reason for their journey. Standing and gazing in wonderment, the Child smiled at them. People started coming in to see the Babe and bringing Him gifts. These gifts were many, and placing them around the manger made it hard for people to see Him. So, Nicholas and Big Red started to move the gifts out of the way placing them under the fur tree in the corner to create a path for all to come and see this Child. There were shepherds, farmers, shopkeepers, and even kings gathered to see the Baby. They came from all corners of the world; all traveled following the star. Even the animals gathered to welcome this Child.

Nicholas and Big Red knew their task was finished. Their reason for the journey was completed. They packed the cart and headed back north. On the journey back to the village and forest of Reinland, they decided to work together making toys for the children of Nicholas' village and the surrounding villages. One day, when they were still several miles from the Reinland Forest, they suddenly heard a high-pitched voice yelling for help. As they followed the voice, it grew louder and louder. They soon realized that the voice was coming from a large hole in the ground. Inside the hole was a small man with a beard and pointed ears.

"An Elf!" shouted Big Red to Nicholas. "I have heard of them, but I have never seen one before."

"Please help me out of this hole," said the Elf. "I have been down here for almost a day now and can't get out."

Big Red lowered his head into the hole and told the Elf to grab onto his antlers and he would pull him out.

"Oh, thank you, thank you!" said the grateful Elf. "Thank you so very much for getting me out of that hole. Hi! Hi! I am Ralph, Ralph the Elf. Ralph is my first name. Ralph the Elf is my last."

"You are welcome," said Big Red. "How did you manage to fall in such a large hole?"

Ralph, Ralph the Elf answered, "It was covered over. A trap it was. I did not see it." Ralph continued, "For saving me, I am indebted to you both. As leader of the Elf village, if you ever need anything, anything at all, just call my name into the wind and we shall come to help."

Nicholas now spoke, "Well, thank you for that offer Ralph. If we have need of your help, we shall call. You must be hungry though, please join us. We were about to stop and rest when we heard you call out."

So, the three sat and ate, and talked for quite some time. Ralph told them of his hidden village on the northwest edge of the Reinland Forest. Nicholas and Big Red told Ralph of their journey following the star, and seeing the special Child born. Ralph explained he heard an Angel speak of the birth of a Savior.

"As far as I know, the entire world heard this Angel proclaim the birth of the Christ Child," said Ralph.

After eating and resting, they said goodbye, parting ways. Ralph shouted as they grew further apart.

"Don't forget. If you need the Elves' help, just call my name into the wind and we will be there."

Days passed as they traveled up the mountain, following the path next to the creek. They were almost to Big Red's home when they heard a soft, sad whimper. It was low and faint. As they followed the sound, they both shouted out.

"Who is there? Are you alright?"

Just then, they heard a female voice. "Over here, please. I am here!"

As they came around a bend in the path, they saw a young doe caught in bear trap. Her front leg was trapped and blood trickled down it. It was cut deeply. Nicholas sprang quickly to her aid, opened the trap and carefully lifted her leg out.

"There now, you are free, but it needs to be cleaned and

bandaged. Let me get my sack," said Nicholas.

As he cleaned and bandaged her hoof she noticed Big Red for the first time and exclaimed, "Oh my! You're, you're a reindeer!"

"A *what* deer?" asked Big Red.

"A reindeer from the Reinland Forest are you not?" replied the doe.

"Yes, I am, but I have never thought of us as reindeer," said Bid Red.

"My name is Big Red, and this fellow helping you is Nicholas."

The doe spoke, "Hello, my name is Adrianna. I have been traveling a long time searching for, well, for you and your kind. We have heard many stories of the Guardians of the Forest, the reindeer, as we call you. I always believed you were real, even though where I come from your kind are just legends. But, here you are! I have found you, or should I say, you have found me."

"Yes, we have, and thankfully, we found you before the hunters returned to check their trap," agreed Nicholas.

Just then, Big Red came closer to Adrianna and spoke quietly to her. "Your leg will take a few weeks to heal. Please let me help you into our cart. Come with us to where I live in the Reinland Forest."

"Thank you for your help. I would love to," said Adrianna.

For the next few days, they continued to follow the path up the mountain. Big Red and Adrianna got to know each other very well on this journey. They talked about everything that interested them, and about their families. During this time of getting to know one another, Adrianna and Big Red started to fall in love.

When they reached the Reinland Forest where Big Red's family and friends were, they all came out and greeted them. Big Red's mother was happy to see her boy and to meet this lovely doe, who she saw he had fallen in love with. She was overjoyed to hear they wanted to get married. All the reindeer there were shocked to see a man with him, especially a man who understood what they all were saying.

After the introductions, they ate and rested. While Big Red helped Nicholas build a hut and a workshop to make the toys, Big Red's mother and Adrianna were preparing for the wedding. It was a beautiful and joyous wedding. They danced, celebrated, and shared stories of their journey following the Star and seeing the Child. They all spoke of that day He was born and that all the creatures could hear the Angel proclaim the birth. The wedding was successful.

Now as the years went by, Big Red continued to gather branches and strip the bark so Nicholas could make toys. When enough toys were made they set out in the sleigh pulled by Big Red to deliver them. All the children of the villages loved seeing Nicholas and Big Red, and all the different toys they brought. In every village, the children all gathered to greet them. Parties and great feasts were prepared. They all gathered in the square after the feast to hear the story of their journey to see the Child being born. None ever tired hearing the story. After a good nights' rest, Nicholas always promised to return.

As time passed, Adrianna and Big Red had many children. The first two fawns born were male twins. When the first twin was born and his hoofs hit the cold snow, he started to dart quickly back and forth to keep his feet from getting cold.

Adrianna saw this, laughed and said, "Look at him dashing about! We shall call him Dasher."

"Yes, I like that," said Big Red, and he continued, "Look at the other one. He looks like he is dancing to keep warm. Let's call him Dancer". Adrianna agreed. The following year when the next fawn was born, Big Red watched him and said,

"Look at him lifting his hooves from the snow. He looks like he is prancing. We shall call him Prancer."

"That's a wonderful name!" said Adrianna.

Big Red and Adrianna's family continued to grow. The next fawn was a female, and to keep warm, she jumped up on Big Red's back.

"Oh, she is going to be a lover; a real vixen she is!" Big Red exclaimed. And so, she was named Vixen. The next two born were again male twins. The first of the two was Comet. He got his name because when his hooves hit the snow he took off running so fast that his white tail looked like the tail of a comet streaking across the night sky. His twin was named Cupid because on his chest he had a birth mark that looked like Cupid's bow and arrow. The following year on the night of a terrible storm the next set of twin reindeer were born. As they were born a bright bolt of lightning and a loud crash of thunder struck. Nicholas entered the barn dripping wet to see how Adrianna was doing just as they were born.

"My goodness," said Nicholas. "These two were born at the peak of this storm. We should name them Donner and Blitzen. That means thunder and lightning in my language."

Adrianna and Big Red both agreed they liked those names, and so they were named Donner and Blitzen.

A few more years went by and the eight young reindeer grew to be healthy and strong. One year when Nicholas told Big Red they had enough toys to be delivered, Big Red asked if he could wait a few days because he wasn't feeling well enough to pull the sleigh. Nicholas agreed, but he knew the village children would be sad, yet they would understand. Just then Comet came running and shouting.

"Father, Uncle Nicholas, we can pull the sleigh. All eight of us can pull it up the mountains and to the villages if you harness us together! We want to help, and would love to visit the villages and meet the children."

By the time he was finished asking, the other seven showed up all shouting.

"Father, please; please can we? We can do it. We can pull the sleigh filled with toys. Please?!"

Big Red, Adrianna, and Nicholas agreed. They harnessed the eight young

reindeer together and off they went up the mountain. All the villages loved

meeting Big Red's children. Parties where thrown in each village and the

toys delivered. Everyone had a grand time, especially Big Red's children.

As they were about to head out from the last village they visited, the

children could hear Nicholas shout,

"Let's head home. On Dasher, Dancer, Prancer and Vixen!

On Comet, Cupid, Donner and Blitzen."

And they took off down the mountain path to home. That night they

reached home and were settled in for a well-deserved nights' rest, when

the Angel appeared again and spoke to them all.

"Nicholas, Big Red, and family, the Son of Man, the Babe you visited

so long ago has completed His task for now here on Earth. For your

kindness and generosity that you have shown to Him and to all of

mankind, the Lord wishes to proclaim you, Nicholas Claus, a saint.

And with sainthood comes eternal life among mankind. You shall

not age nor shall your family, and that includes Big Red, Adrianna, and their children. Nicholas you shall deliver toys to all good children of the world, every year to mark the birth date of our Lord and Savior, Jesus Christ. And from this day forward, that day shall be known as Christmas, a day of joy and prayer for all. It will be a day of giving and loving one another as He has loved you. Peace to all on this earth and good will. And to the eight children of Adrianna and Big Red, the Lord bestows upon you the gift of flight, so that the task of delivering toys around the world shall be made easier."

Then the Angel vanished! Big Red and Nicholas looked at each other not knowing what to say. They could not believe that the Baby they saw just 33 years ago had died. They knew inside that this was not something sad, but the start of something extraordinary, amazing, and joyous, a new beginning for all mankind.

They knew that He was in a special place, preparing it for us. It is a place of understanding, great peace, and love. He is there to welcome us when it is time to go to our true home, Heaven.

As they looked around Nicholas said, "How are we going to build enough toys for all the good children of the world every year?" Big Red had that same question. All afternoon they pondered. Finally, Nicholas had an idea. He turned into the direction of the wind and shouted,

"Ralph, Ralph the Elf, we need your help!"

A moment later they heard a rustling coming from the forest. When they turned to look, there was Ralph, Ralph the Elf and hundreds of elves coming out of the forest.

"I heard my name in the wind and knew you needed us. So here we are, here to help you make the toys for the children. The Angel came to us and told us what we needed to do when you called," Ralph said to Nicholas.

That entire night they talked and worked on the details to create a great workshop. It would be one that would be large enough to allow hundreds of elves plenty of room to build toys. They were trying to decide where to build this workshop when Big Red spoke up.

"I have the perfect place. A place where we shall not be disturbed, room enough to build a workshop, and a village for all of us to live. It's also a place where you, Nicholas, can see all the children of the world. The North Pole!"

"What an excellent idea! The perfect place! We shall leave in the morning," Nicholas proclaimed.

That next morning, they gathered all the tools, supplies, and everything they needed and headed out for the North Pole, where, to this day, they all live building toys for all the good boys and girls.

Now the first year they were to deliver the toys from the North Pole, the elves and Big Red were working to harness the eight reindeer to the great sleigh. Nicholas came out of his house wearing a new suit, walked over to Big Red and said,

"I chose this color suit to honor you, my old friend. I am saddened that you will not be traveling with me to deliver the toys. From this day on I will represent you in spirit by wearing a bright red suit every year."

Big Red just smiled and nodded.

A few years later, Adrianna and Big Red had another baby. The day before he was born Big Red confided to Adrianna that he always had a secret desire that one of his children would be born like him with shiny, bright red fur. Well, when that baby reindeer was born, he was born with something bright, shiny and red, but it wasn't his fur. Can you guess who that was?

INSPIRATION

My wife Adrian and I live in a small town in East Texas. She is a 3rd grade teacher and I drive an 18 wheeler throughout the state. Christmas has always been an especially joyous time of year for us. I first got the idea for this book when I met Big Red. He is a 26-foot tall reindeer that can be viewed at the Christmas Ranch in Cleveland, Texas. My wife, Adrian, along with our friend Diane, the co-owner of the Christmas Ranch, took a large U-Haul truck to Houston, Texas where they picked up Big Red. He was a giant Christmas display that used to be at a mall in Texas. The mall donated it to a non-profit organization where Diane found it and purchased it so they could display him at the entrance of the Christmas Ranch. Every year Bob and Diane Hanley open their property to visitors who drive through and see a display of over a quarter of a million lights. With the help of family and friends, they start setting up the first weekend of November and the lights come on for all to enjoy Thanksgiving night. They have been doing this for over 30 years. They do it for the joy it brings children and their parents. My wife and I have had the privilege of helping with many others at the Christmas Ranch for several years, which has inspired me to tell the story of Big Red. We hope you enjoyed reading this story as much as we have writing it.

Like us on Facebook: www.facebook.com/bigred26footreindeer

Made in the USA
Columbia, SC
30 December 2021